The Missing Mommy Cure

Helps Relieve Separation Anxiety

Midge Leavey

Illustrations by Irened Olds

AuthorHouse
1663 Liberty Drive
Bloomington, IN 47403
www.authorhouse.com
Phone: 1-800-839-8640

Published by AuthorHouse 04/04/2013

ISBN: 978-1-4817-3494-3 (sc)
978-1-4817-3495-0 (e)

Library of Congress Control Number: 2013906108

I would like to dedicate this book to my sons, T.J. and Jack, for introducing some of the struggles mom's go through which led me to writing this book.

To my husband George for always supporting me.

To my friends Beverly, Linda and Laura for their positive and negative feedback.

and to my networking group for their kind words and support.

It's time for school and I didn't have a clue
I didn't want to leave mommy, I didn't know what to do

So I told Mommy how I felt inside
My stomach flipped and I wanted to hide

My mom smiled and said she had just the cure
as she flew open her dresser drawer

as I watched mommy, I dried my teary eyes
and held back my quivering chin and boastful sighs

Mommy looked through her dresser drawer some more
Hoping to find my "missing her" cure

"What is it mommy? I cannot wait!
I hope it's a puppy! That would be great!"

"Or is it an elephant from the zoo?
Or a scary ghost that says boo?"

No she said, "It is not a ghost or elephant from the zoo,
This is much more important to me and you!"

Mom pulled out a magic wristband
My excitement was more than I could withstand

She smiled and said with a familiar sigh
This magic band will help you say goodbye

It will help you learn and play along
Reminding yourself that you can be strong
With a smile and a hug on went the magic band
She placed it on my wrist and over my hand

Miss Midgies
PRESCHOOL

This band, my dear, will help you through your day
There is no need to be sad while you learn and play

Thank you mommy, I will not be sad anymore while we are separated
Our magic band reminds me of the bond we created!

The End

Play this fun game with your child!
Help your child find 12 hidden wristbands in the picture!
B
A
C
D
2
1

Go to: www.missmidgiesbooks.com to order your very own "Missing Mommy Cure" wristband.

Printed in Great Britain
by Amazon